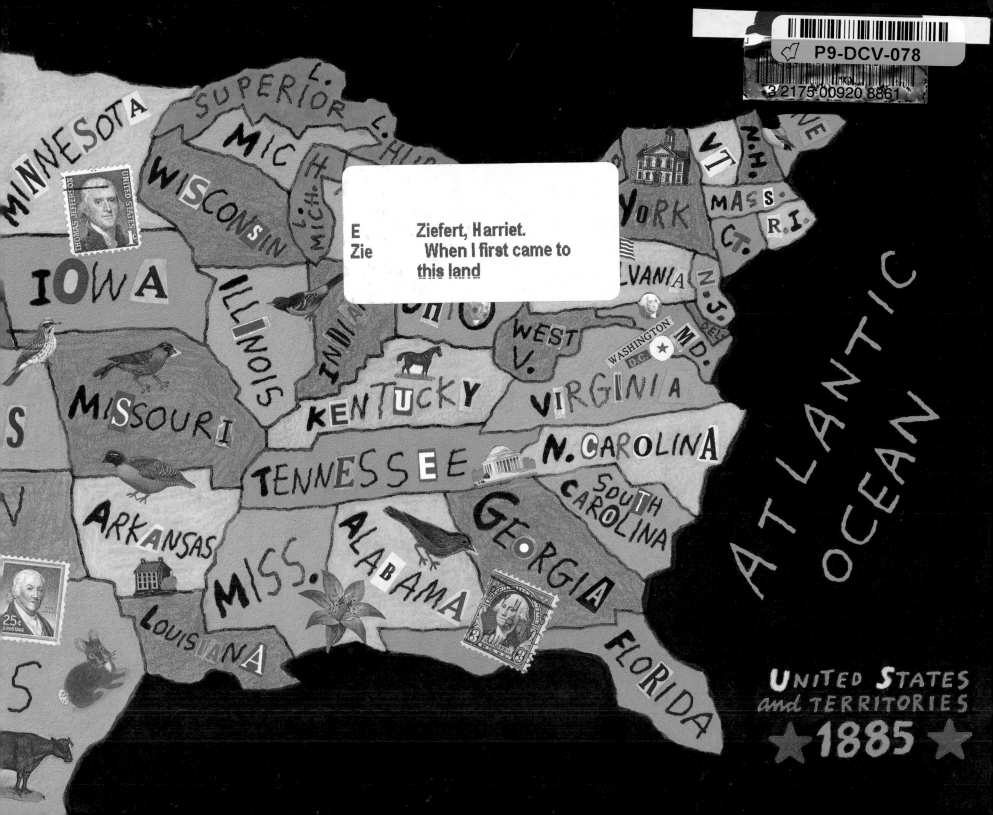

E
Zie

Ziefert, Harriet.
When I first came to
this land

MINNESOTA

L. SUPERIOR

L. HURON

MICH.

Mich.

WISCONSIN

IOWA

ILLINOIS

INDIANA

OHIO

VT

N.H.

MASS.

R.I.

YORK

CT.

PENNSYLVANIA

N.J.

DEL.

WEST V.

WASHINGTON D.C.

MD.

VIRGINIA

MISSOURI

KENTUCKY

TENNESSEE

N. CAROLINA

SOUTH CAROLINA

ARKANSAS

MISS.

ALABAMA

GEORGIA

LOUISIANA

FLORIDA

UNITED STATES

1c

25c S.POSTAGE

3c

ATLANTIC OCEAN

UNITED STATES
and TERRITORIES
★ 1885 ★

In memory of my grandparents,
who came here from Russia—HMZ

For Leon—ST

G. P. PUTNAM'S SONS

A division of Penguin Young Readers Group.
Published by The Penguin Group.

Penguin Group (USA) Inc., 375 Hudson Street, New York, NY 10014, U.S.A.
Penguin Group (Canada), 90 Eglinton Avenue East, Suite 700, Toronto, Ontario, Canada M4P 2Y3 (a division of Pearson Penguin Canada Inc.).
Penguin Books Ltd, 80 Strand, London WC2R 0RL, England. Penguin Ireland, 25 St. Stephen's Green, Dublin 2, Ireland (a division of Penguin Books Ltd.).
Penguin Group (Australia), 250 Camberwell Road, Camberwell, Victoria 3124, Australia (a division of Pearson Australia Group Pty Ltd).
Penguin Books India Pvt Ltd, 11 Community Centre, Panchsheel Park, New Delhi - 110 017, India.
Penguin Group (NZ), Cnr Airborne and Rosedale Roads, Albany, Auckland 1310, New Zealand (a division of Pearson New Zealand Ltd).
Penguin Books (South Africa) (Pty) Ltd, 24 Sturdee Avenue, Rosebank, Johannesburg 2196, South Africa. Penguin Books Ltd, Registered Offices: 80 Strand, London WC2R 0RL, England.

WHEN I FIRST CAME TO THIS LAND
Words & Music by Oscar Brand
TRO–© Copyright 1957 (Renewed), 1965 (Renewed)
Ludlow Music, Inc., New York, NY
Used by Permission

Text copyright © 1998 by Harriet Ziefert. Illustrations copyright © 1998 by Simms Taback.

Published simultaneously in Canada. Manufactured in China by South China Printing Co. Ltd. Text set in Cheltenham Bold.

Library of Congress Cataloging-in-Publication Data
Ziefert, Harriet. When I first came to this land / retold by Harriet Ziefert; pictures by Simms Taback. p. cm. Summary: Illustrations and words to a traditional song describe the adventures
of a pioneer who buys a farm and builds life for himself and his family. 1. Folk songs, English—United States—Texts. [1. Folk songs—United States.] I. Taback, Simms, ill. II. Title.
PZ8.3.Z49Wf 1998 782.42162'13'00833—DC21 97-9612 CIP AC
ISBN 978-0-399-24793-4
5 7 9 10 8 6 4

WHEN I FIRST CAME TO THIS LAND

Based on a song by Oscar Brand

RETOLD BY HARRIET ZIEFERT
PICTURES BY SIMMS TABACK

G. P. Putnam's Sons

When I first came to this land,
I was not a wealthy man.

But the land was sweet and good,
And I did what I could.

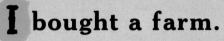 bought a farm.

And I called my farm
Muscle-in-my-arm!

I borrowed a plow.

I called my plow
Don't-know-how!
And I called my farm
Muscle-in-my-arm!

I bought a horse.

I called my horse
I'm-the-boss!
I called my plow
Don't-know-how!
And I called my farm
Muscle-in-my-arm!

I built a shack.

I called my shack
Break-my-back!
I called my horse
I'm-the-boss!
I called my plow
Don't-know-how!
And I called my farm
Muscle-in-my-arm!

I bought a cow.

I called my cow
No-milk-now!
I called my shack
Break-my-back!
I called my horse
I'm-the-boss!
I called my plow
Don't-know-how!
And I called my farm
Muscle-in-my-arm!

I bought a pig.

I called my pig
Too-darn-big!
I called my cow
No-milk-now!
I called my shack
Break-my-back!
I called my horse
I'm-the-boss!
I called my plow
Don't-know-how!
And I called my farm
Muscle-in-my-arm!

I found a wife.

I called my wife
Spice-of-my-life!
I called my pig
Too-darn-big!
I called my cow
No-milk-now!
I called my shack
Break-my-back!
I called my horse
I'm-the-boss!
I called my plow
Don't-know-how!
And I called my farm
Muscle-in-my-arm!

I had a son.

I called my son
So-much-fun!
I called my wife
Spice-of-my-life!
I called my pig
Too-darn-big!
I called my cow
No-milk-now!
I called my shack
Break-my-back!
I called my horse
I'm-the-boss!
I called my plow
Don't-know-how!
And I called my farm
Muscle-in-my-arm!

My son found a duck.

And he called his duck
Duck-Duck-Duck!
And he called his pa
Da-Da-Da!
And he called his ma
Ma-Ma-Ma!

When I first came to this land,
I was not a wealthy man.

But the land was sweet and good,
And I did what I could!